WHY DOESN'T THE EARTH FALL UP?

Also by Vicki Cobb

Fuzz Does It!
Gobs of Goo
Lots of Rot
The Monsters Who Died
More Power to You!
The Scoop on Ice Cream
Skyscraper Going Up!
Sneakers Meet Your Feet
The Trip of a Drip

WHY DOESN'T THE EARTH FALL UP?

and other not such dumb questions about motion

BY VICKI COBB

illustrated by Ted Enik

LODESTAR BOOKS   E. P. DUTTON   NEW YORK

for Christine Tomasino

Library of Congress Cataloging-in-Publication Data

Cobb, Vicki.
  Why doesn't the earth fall up? and other not such dumb
questions about motion / by Vicki Cobb; illustrated by Ted
Enik.—1st ed.
    p. cm.
  Summary: Answers nine questions about motion,
explaining Newton's Laws of Motion; gravity; centrifugal
force; and other principles of movement.
  ISBN 0-525-67253-2
  1. Motion—Miscellanea—Juvenile literature. [1. Motion.
2. Questions and answers.] I. Enik, Ted, ill. II. Title.
QC127.4.C63 1988   88-11108
531′.11—dc19   CIP
                                              AC

Published in the United States by
E. P. Dutton, New York, N.Y.,
a division of NAL Penguin Inc.

Published simultaneously in Canada by
Fitzhenry & Whiteside Limited, Toronto

Editor: Virginia Buckley

Printed in the U.S.A.   First Edition
10 9 8 7 6 5 4 3 2 1

Contents

Why Does a Rolling Ball Stop Rolling?

A rolling ball, especially one rolling on level ground, should never stop. Do this experiment to see why:

Give a ball a little push so it rolls up a hill. Watch it roll slower and slower until it stops for a moment, then rolls back downhill. Now, watch how the ball rolls downhill. It goes faster and faster. Think about this: If the ball rolling uphill slows down, and the ball rolling downhill speeds up, how should it roll if there is no hill? A ball rolling on level ground should not speed up or slow down. It should go at the same speed forever!

But that's not what happens in real life. Balls rolling on level ground do come to a stop sooner or later. Something must be stopping them. What is it?

A man named Isaac Newton thought about this more than 300 years ago. It's obvious that a resting ball will rest forever. It will remain resting until it is hit by some outside force that will make it move. That's easy to understand. But Newton figured that this same rule is true for balls that are in motion. Once a ball is moving, it will keep on moving forever unless it is stopped by some force. In other words, just as a push or pull is needed to make resting objects *start* moving, a push or a pull is needed to make moving objects *stop* moving.

Any ball that stops rolling must have a force stopping it. What is it? It's not a force that's easy to see. As it turns out, the force that slows the ball acts at the point where the ball touches the surface it's rolling on. This force is called *friction*. Friction is a force that occurs between two surfaces where there is motion. It works against that motion. If you could design a machine without friction, it would move forever. Many have tried to make such a perpetual-motion machine. All have failed.

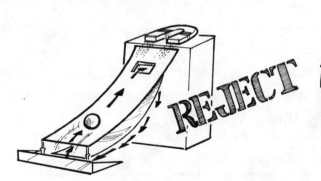

Newton's answer to this dumb question explains why all balls and other nonliving objects either move or don't move. It is called Newton's first law of motion:

Moving objects will move forever, and resting objects will rest forever, unless some outside force acts on them.

How Do We Know the Earth Is Moving When It Looks as if the Sky Is Moving?

How do you know when you are moving? You feel bumps and shakes. You feel the wind in your face and see the scenery passing by.

Now suppose that your ride is perfectly smooth and there is no wind. Imagine that you are in a boat in the middle of a perfectly calm sea. Another boat is passing in the distance. How would you know that you are moving, or that you are still and the other boat is moving past you? The answer is that you would have no way of knowing. You could be moving or you could only appear to be moving.

This was the problem that faced early astronomers. They saw the sun move across the sky by day, and the stars move across by night. They saw the moon rise and set. It was easier to think that the earth was not moving and everything else in the heavens moved around it. After all, that's the way it looks.

Almost 2,000 years ago, a Greek astronomer named Ptolemy (TAHL-a-me) said that the earth was the center of the universe and the moon, sun, stars, and planets all moved around it. Travelers needed to know where the heavenly bodies would be, since they used them to find their way. Ptolemy predicted correctly enough where they could be found. His system was used for 1,400 years.

About 450 years ago, a Polish astronomer named Copernicus (Co-PER-ni-cuss) had a different idea. Ptolemy made some mistakes predicting where planets would be. Copernicus figured that the universe would be a lot simpler if all the planets, including the earth, moved around the sun.

At first, this idea of Copernicus's was not popular. It went against what people saw with their own eyes. Telescopes had not yet been invented. Copernicus had no proof that the earth moved. But he knew what the proof would be.

The stars are grouped into well-known patterns called *constellations*. Constellations, like the Big Dipper, seem to be always the same. Copernicus believed that some of the stars in a constellation were closer to earth than others. He believed that the patterns of the stars changed a tiny bit as the earth moved around the sun. This change, he thought, proved that the earth moved.

COPERNICUS

Here's how you can see what Copernicus meant. Hold your pointed index finger about one foot in front of your nose. Look at your finger as you open and close each eye in turn. See how the background shifts position behind your finger. This is because each eye sees the background from a different position.

Copernicus predicted that certain stars in a constellation would appear closer together at one time of year than they would six months later. In six months the earth has moved halfway around the sun. It is as far away as it can get from its position six months earlier. Some stars are closer to earth than others. So the distances between stars appear to change as the earth moves, just as the background shifts behind your finger as you switch eyes. Copernicus knew that the apparent change in the distances between the stars would be tiny. It would be hard to see because the stars were so far away. But after the telescope was invented, astronomers measured the changing patterns of the stars as the earth moved. We now have our proof.

But the motion of the earth around the sun does not explain how the sun rises and sets. So Copernicus said that the earth has two kinds of motion. The earth also spins like a top while it is traveling around the sun. The spinning of the earth makes the sun appear to move across the sky by day, and it makes the starry sky rise and set at night.

THE EARTH SPINS JUST OVER 365 TIMES FOR EVERY TRIP AROUND THE SUN.

THAT LITTLE EXTRA SPIN ADDS UP. EVERY FOUR YEARS IT EQUALS A WHOLE DAY. THEN WE HAVE A YEAR WITH 366 DAYS.

IT'S CALLED LEAP YEAR. LEAP YEAR DAY IS FEBRUARY 29.

If the Earth Is Spinning, Why Don't We Feel It Move?

We don't feel the earth move because it is spinning at a steady rate—so the ride is smooth. We feel motion only when there is a change in the way we are moving. And a change in motion occurs only when an outside force acts on us. (Remember Newton's first law.)

Everything on the earth's surface is moving with the earth. Check this out: The next time you ride in a car, ask the driver to go at a steady speed. Drop a pencil on the floor while you are moving. Later, when the car is not moving, drop the pencil exactly the same way. Both times it will land on the same spot. The motion of the car does not change the fall of the pencil, as long as that motion is steady. Only a sudden change in the car's motion while you are dropping the pencil will change where the pencil ends up.

When you are sitting in a moving car, you have the same forward movement as the car. If the car suddenly crashes to a stop, you keep this forward motion and can be thrown through the windshield.

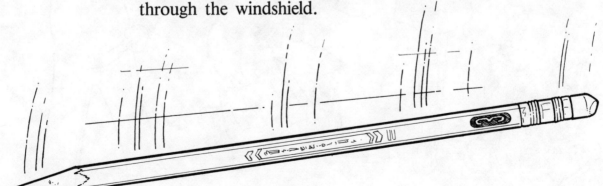

Which Falls Faster, a Bowling Ball or a Marble?

The idea that heavier objects fall faster than lighter ones is one of those great mistakes that people believed for centuries. An ancient Greek named Aristotle (AR-is-tot-ul) was the first to write this theory down. Aristotle said that if one stone weighed ten pounds, and another stone weighed one pound, the ten-pound stone would fall ten times faster.

Aristotle was a very important thinker and writer. Many people believed Aristotle was right about everything. No one tested his ideas.

It's easy to test the idea that heavy objects fall faster than light ones. You can try it yourself with a friend. One of you should drop two objects of different weights at the same time. You might drop them off a porch or jungle gym. Have your friend stand on the ground at a safe distance to see which one reaches the ground first. You should get a tie every time.

A man who experimented with how things fall lived about 2,000 years after Aristotle. He was an Italian named Galileo (Ga-li-LAY-oh). There is a story that Galileo dropped two different weights off the Leaning Tower of Pisa, which may or may not be true. But we do know that Galileo was very clever in the way he measured how things fall.

When Galileo lived, about 400 years ago, there were no watches or clocks. Any falling object fell too fast for him to measure how long it took. So Galileo decided to slow down falling objects. Instead of dropping objects off buildings, he decided to roll balls down a ramp. He figured that the same force that made things fall would make balls roll down a ramp. This force is called *gravity*. A ramp would make it easier to see gravity in action. He measured the time by catching drops of water while a ball rolled. He could change the steepness of the ramp and measure the distance the ball traveled while water dripped. The steepest ramp is very close to a free-fall.

Galileo did lots of experiments. He made an incredible discovery. No matter how heavy or light they are, all balls fall toward earth at the same rate!

Galileo also discovered how to ask questions that could be answered by experiments in his laboratory. This is the way scientists collect information. For this reason, Galileo is called the father of modern science.

Why Can't You Stand an Egg on Its End?

THE ONLY WAY YOU CAN STAND AN EGG ON ITS END IS TO GIVE IT A SUPPORT THAT CAN OVERCOME GRAVITY.

AS LONG AS YOUR CENTER OF GRAVITY IS LINED UP OVER YOUR FEET, YOU WON'T FALL.

KEEPING YOUR CENTER OF GRAVITY LINED UP OVER YOUR FEET IS A BALANCING ACT.

You can't stand an egg on its end because of the way gravity makes things fall. Gravity is a force of attraction between the earth and objects on or near its surface. When gravity pulls on the ball, it is as if the center of the earth is attracting the center of the ball. An egg doesn't have a regular shape like a ball. So gravity pulls on the point of the egg that seems to be its center. This spot is called the egg's *center of gravity*.

An egg's center of gravity is not at the center of the egg.

An object falls toward the center of the earth. It would keep going if there were a hole to fall into. It is as if the object were trying to get its center of gravity as close to the earth's center of gravity as possible. An egg will rest on its side because its curved surface makes it easy to move. And when it rolls on its side its center of gravity is as low as it can get.

Why Doesn't the Moon Fall to Earth?

Gravity is the force pulling the moon and the earth together, just as gravity is the force pulling an egg and the earth together. If gravity were the only force acting on the moon, it would crash into the earth. The moon doesn't fall into the earth because there's an equal force sending the moon off into space.

This force comes from the motion of the moon. If gravity suddenly disappeared, the moon would fly off in a straight line. Imagine whirling a ball at the end of a string. The string is a force holding the ball in its path around the center, just like gravity acts on the moon. When you let go, the ball flies off in a straight line. If you wanted to make the whirling ball fly to a target, you would have to time your release very accurately.

The combination of the force toward the center and the motion of the whirling object seems to create another force. It is called *centrifugal force,* meaning "away from the center." Actually, centrifugal force is the absence of a force toward the center. You can feel centrifugal force sending blood into your fingertips when you swing your arms in a circle. Your arms won't fly off because they're attached to your body. Your blood is loose, so it starts to move off into space until it is stopped by your fingertips. Whirling your arms is a good way to warm your hands in winter.

Gravity and the motion of the moon work together to trap the moon into a circular path around the earth. This path is called an *orbit*.

Isaac Newton figured out why the moon doesn't fall into the earth. There is a story about this discovery. Newton was lying under an apple tree, thinking about the moon. He was wondering why it wasn't falling. An apple fell from the tree. Newton looked at the falling apple and suddenly realized that the moon *is* falling. But the fall is constantly being stopped by the moon's straight-line motion into space.

The moon keeps moving because there is no friction to slow it down. If there were no forces acting on the moon, its motion would carry it out of our solar system. Gravity constantly keeps the direction of the moon's motion in a circular orbit.

NEWTON'S UPDATED First Law of Motion: MOVING OBJECTS WILL KEEP MOVING FOREVER IN A STRAIGHT LINE, and RESTING OBJECTS WILL REST FOREVER, UNLESS SOME OUTSIDE FORCE ACTS ON THEM.

Newton added this idea—how forces can change the direction of motion—to his first law of motion: Moving objects will keep moving forever *in a straight line,* and resting objects will rest forever, unless some outside force acts on them.

The same forces keep man-made satellites in orbit. Space engineers figure that a satellite has to go about five miles each second to stay in an orbit about a hundred miles from the earth's surface. A speed of seven miles each second is fast enough to escape the pull of the earth's gravity and send a spacecraft into space.

We Say That an Apple Falls Down to Earth.
Why Doesn't the Earth Fall Up to the Apple?

Believe it or not, the earth is falling up to the apple with the same force as the apple falling down to earth. Since the earth is so huge by comparison, you can't see the earth's attraction to the apple.

Isaac Newton was the first person to think about this so-called dumb question. When Newton saw the apple fall and thought about the moon falling to earth, he began to really think about gravity. Newton said that gravity was a force of attraction between objects. Every bit of matter has gravity and is attracted to every other bit of matter. This pull can go across space. So the apple pulls the earth up as the earth pulls the apple down. But gravity is a very weak force. It isn't felt unless you have a huge amount of matter gathered together in a body as big as the earth or the moon. Newton's idea about gravity is that gravity pulls the earth and moon together, just as it pulls the earth and apple together.

The apple is so small and has so little gravity that it's impossible to detect its pull on earth. But the pull of the moon's gravity causes the tides of the ocean. The water on earth is falling *up* toward the moon!

Newton summed up his ideas about gravity being a two-way street in his third law of motion:

Every action has an equal and opposite reaction.

WHEN I HIT THE WALL, THE WALL STOPS MY FIST WITH AN EQUAL FORCE. **OUCH!**

THE AIR SPEEDING OUT OF THE BACK OF A BALLOON SENDS THE BALLOON FORWARD. SORT OF.

NEWTON'S **THIRD** LAW OF MOTION: EVERY ACTION HAS AN **EQUAL** AND **OPPOSITE** REACTION

Which Takes Longer, a Big, High Swing or a Small, Low Swing?

EVERYONE KNOWS A BIG, HIGH SWING TAKES LONGER.

LITTLE, SHORT SWINGS ARE NOT EXCITING. THEY PUT ME TO SLEEP. PERSONALLY, I LIKE TO GET PUSHED ON A SWING.

You can do an experiment to answer this question. Go with a friend to a playground that has swings. Have your friend start counting at a steady rate the moment you give an empty swing a good hard push. You friend should count with his or her back to the swing. At the end of the fifth swing, tell your friend to stop counting.

Now repeat your experiment. But this time give the swing a tiny push, just enough to set it swinging back and forth. Again, tell your friend to stop counting after five swings. Did your friend count to almost the same number each time? Keep on experimenting. What happens when you count ten high swings and ten low ones? What happens when you use a watch with a second hand instead of a friend who counts? What happens when someone is sitting on the swing?

Your experiment will help you discover that a big swing takes exactly the same amount of time as a small swing!

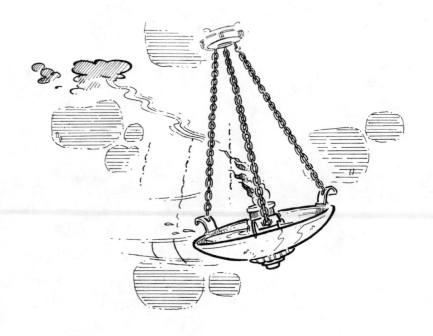

Galileo discovered this rule for a swinging object. One day he was in church. A lamplighter had just lit a lamp that was hanging from the ceiling. It was swinging back and forth. Galileo wondered if a big swing would take longer than a little swing. Since he didn't have a watch or a friend to count for him, he used his own heartbeat. Galileo felt his pulse as he counted lamp swings. He discovered that the lamp always took the same amount of time to swing back and forth, even though the swings got smaller and smaller.

What Is a Swinging Object Good For?

A freely swinging object is called a *pendulum*. A pendulum swings with a regular beat. Why not use it to measure time? Remember, in the days of Galileo there were no clocks or watches as we know them. Galileo had to measure short amounts of time by catching drips of water. A pendulum became another way to count short bits of time.

At first, pendulums were used only to time people's pulses. Later, inventors used pendulums to make all kinds of clocks.

A pendulum can also prove that the earth turns. In 1851, French scientist Jean Foucault hung an iron-ball pendulum from the top of a dome in a large building. Marks on the floor made it seem as if the swinging pendulum slowly changed direction. Actually it was swinging back and forth in a straight line. The earth was turning underneath the pendulum.

Index

X

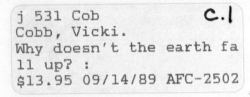